My Brown Papa

by Crystal K Thornburg

Illustrations by Emily Hercock

My Brown Papa
Copyright © 2021 by Crystal K. Thornburg

Illustrations by: Emily Hercock
Cover Designed by AuthorTree
Interior Book Formatting by AuthorTree

Independently published.

To my sons Hunter and Hatcher.
To Elmore Bryant Jr. (The best papa) and to my
husband David who encouraged me to follow my dream.

Papa...Papa...
Oh, hey there!

You see my papa there in the blue shirt?
Yeah, he's an extraordinary papa.

But, me, I'm just a simple kid.

My name is Sam.
I have a kid brother named Sid.

Yeah, that's him trying to race to our Papa. Like any other kid brother, he is annoying as heck.

You may have noticed that my papa looks a little different from me. Have you asked yourself that question yet?

How come our papa is brown and my brother and I are white? People ask us the same dumb question all the time.
"Why is your papa black and you and your brother are white?"

People squint their eyes and say, "How can that happen?"

Now, I know you have heard your teachers say, "There's no such thing as a dumb question but, for me, those questions are dumb because I can't see myself not having my papa. Even if he were green, he'd still be the best papa in the world.

You can tell from my picture that I like basketball. My papa is my biggest fan. He comes to all my games and cheers louder than all the other grandparents.

Sometimes it's pretty funny because he's yelling my name and screaming for me to shoot more points.

I try my very best to score just for him because he gets so excited.

Papa loves basketball just like me but there is something else we like to do together.

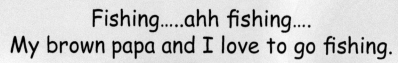
Fishing.....ahh fishing....
My brown papa and I love to go fishing.

One time my papa told me a story about a time when he was not able to go certain places or eat at restaurants.

He couldn't even drink from a water fountain, only from the ones that said, "BLACKS ONLY." Can you believe that? He told me he was so glad that people like Martin Luther King helped changed those laws.

He pulled me in tight and said, "Long time ago, I couldn't be your papa."

I thought I saw a tear come from his eye. And guess what? One did come from mine because ME living without my papa... well, I think... I would just CRY.

The next day when I saw my brown papa, I wanted to know why he couldn't eat at restaurants cause we love to go to this place called Nicks.

I especially like to go with him because, like any other extraordinary papa, I can get whatever I want.

Momma says I have this thing called ADD where I can't stay focused, so try to overlook that and I'll try to stay 'focused' on telling my story.

I think I'm supposed to be telling you about why they wouldn't let my brown papa take the bus or even go to school with white kids.

Something about segregation. I know, right? Who makes up these big words. Segregation happened a long time ago. I'm not going to tell you dates, cause who remembers that anyway.

What we remember is how unfair this thing called segregation was.

Segregation means: that certain groups of people must be separated from others.

So that meant "Black people couldn't go to school with white people." Can you believe that, too? I mean, it must have been totally weird back then.

You know what I learned, too? Black people were not even allowed to ride in the front of the bus. They had to sit in the way back.

Seriously! O M G, people. Do you know that my papa and I took a bus from Columbia, South Carolina to Charlotte, North Carolina to watch a cool basketball game.

Now, just image how dumb that would have been if my papa wasn't allowed to sit by me on the bus. I mean, we made a great memory that I'll remember forever.

Like I told you at the beginning of the story, I have one extraordinary papa, so I guess I should give a great big thanks to Rosa Parks for that one because she was the first African American lady to refuse to sit in the back of the bus.

I hear people made such a fuss that they even put her in jail.

Let's just take a moment of silence and thank our lucky stars that we are cool cats growing up in a world where everyone can ride buses together, go to school together, and eat together 'cause I tell you, I just couldn't live back then.

How about you?

Oh, no, I think my ADD is kicking in and I feel like I want to tell you a million little things about my papa but instead I want you to promise me that you will not choose a book by its cover and never ever judge a person based on skin color.

You get it?

Like the cover of a book might look boring but what's inside the book might be the coolest story you have ever read.

It's the same with a person who may not look like you, talk like you, walk like you, or wear the same cool cat clothes like you, but that person may just be someone extraordinary.

A big thank you to artist Rachel Mangum Wilder for the beautiful painting of papa and the boys!

About The Author

Crystal K. Thornburg was born and raised in Lexington, SC. Crystal considers her faith and family most important. Crystal is an educator and enjoys teaching writing to her students. If she isn't watching her sons play sports, you can find her relaxing on the lake with family and friends. *My Brown Papa* is Crystal's first children's book.

Follow me at:
facebook.com/crystal.thornburg.7
instagram.com/crystal.thornburg.7

CPSIA information can be obtained
at www.ICGtesting.com
Printed in the USA
BVHW020808221021
619555BV00023B/7